Dear Parents:

Congratulations! Your child is taking the first steps on an exciting journey. The destination? Independent reading!

STEP INTO READING® will help your child get there. The program offers five steps to reading success. Each step includes fun stories and colorful art or photographs. In addition to original fiction and books with favorite characters, there are Step into Reading Non-Fiction Readers, Phonics Readers and Boxed Sets, Sticker Readers, and Comic Readers—a complete literacy program with something to interest every child.

Learning to Read, Step by Step!

Ready to Read   Preschool–Kindergarten
• **big type and easy words** • **rhyme and rhythm** • **picture clues**
For children who know the alphabet and are eager to begin reading.

Reading with Help   Preschool–Grade 1
• **basic vocabulary** • **short sentences** • **simple stories**
For children who recognize familiar words and sound out new words with help.

Reading on Your Own   Grades 1–3
• **engaging characters** • **easy-to-follow plots** • **popular topics**
For children who are ready to read on their own.

Reading Paragraphs   Grades 2–3
• **challenging vocabulary** • **short paragraphs** • **exciting stories**
For newly independent readers who read simple sentences with confidence.

Ready for Chapters   Grades 2–4
• **chapters** • **longer paragraphs** • **full-color art**
For children who want to take the plunge into chapter books but still like colorful pictures.

STEP INTO READING® is designed to give every child a successful reading experience. The grade levels are only guides; children will progress through the steps at their own speed, developing confidence in their reading.

Remember, a lifetime love of reading starts with a single step!

Step into Reading, Random House, and the Random House colophon are registered trademarks of Penguin Random House LLC.

Visit us on the Web!
StepIntoReading.com
randomhousekids.com

Educators and librarians, for a variety of teaching tools, visit us at RHTeachersLibrarians.com

ISBN 978-0-7364-3456-0 (trade) — ISBN 978-0-7364-8209-7 (lib. bdg.) —
ISBN 978-0-7364-3457-7 (ebook)

Printed in the United States of America   10 9 8 7 6 5 4 3 2 1

Disney
ZOOTOPIA

THE BIG CASE

by Bill Scollon

illustrated by the Disney Storybook Art Team

Random House 🏠 New York

Judy Hopps is a bunny.
Her parents want her
to be a carrot farmer.
But she dreams of being
a police officer.

Today her dream comes true!
Judy is the first bunny
to join the police force.
In Zootopia,
anyone can be anything!

Judy moves

from Bunnyburrow

to the big city.

The city is exciting and noisy.

It is also very crowded.

But everyone gets along!

Judy will help

keep Zootopia safe.

Judy reports for duty.

She wants to solve crimes.

But her job is

to write parking tickets.

After a busy morning,

she sees a fox.

She thinks he looks sly.

She follows him.

The fox is named Nick Wilde.

Nick tricks Judy

into buying a Jumbo-pop.

Nick uses the Jumbo-pop

to make little pawpsicles.

He sells them to lemmings.

Back at headquarters,
an otter is reported missing.
Judy tells Chief Bogo
and Assistant Mayor Bellwether
she wants the case!

A picture shows the otter

with one of Nick's pawpsicles.

Judy tricks Nick

into helping her

with the case.

Nick and Judy
visit a yak.
He saw the otter
in a car.
He remembers
the license plate number!

Flash is a sloth.

He can find out

who owns the car.

But Flash is very slow!

It takes hours

to get the information.

The information leads
to Manchas the jaguar.
He is the driver
who picked up the otter.

Manchas turns
into a savage beast!
Nick and Judy run
for their lives!

Manchas disappears.

Judy and Nick search videos

of the scene.

They see wolves take Manchas

away in a van.

Nick guesses where they went.

Judy and Nick sneak
into an old hospital.
They find the otter and the jaguar.
There are other
savage animals, too.
A door opens!

It is Mayor Lionheart!

He knew where

the savage animals were!

A doctor tells him that stress

turns the animals

into savage beasts.

Lionheart does not want
the city to panic.
He will keep the animals
locked up.
Judy records Lionheart
on her phone.

Judy and Nick tell Chief Bogo
that the missing animals are
at the old hospital.
Mayor Lionheart is arrested
for kidnapping animals.
Bellwether becomes mayor.

The animals in Zootopia

are afraid.

Who will turn savage next?

Nobody gets along—

not even Judy and Nick.

Judy quits the police force.

Judy goes back to Bunnyburrow.

Her dad tells her

about night howlers.

They are flowers that can make

animals go crazy.

Someone was using them in Zootopia!

Judy returns to Zootopia.

She apologizes to Nick.

She tells Nick that someone

is using night howlers

to make animals turn savage.

Judy and Nick find
a secret night howler lab.
The flowers are being made
into a bright-blue juice!

Judy and Nick
have a plan.
They steal a case
of the night howler juice.

Nick and Judy hurry
to the police station.
Bellwether stops them.
She grabs the case
and forces Nick
to take the night howler juice.

Nick is turning savage!

Bellwether wants

to make everyone afraid.

Then she can control the city.

But Nick is *not* turning savage.
He and Judy switched
the night howler juice
with blueberry juice.
They recorded Bellwether
on Judy's carrot pen.

It was a trick!

Chief Bogo arrests Bellwether.

Case closed!

Nick and Judy make a great team.

They will keep

working together

to keep Zootopia safe!